Let's Make a Pie

by Linda Cernak

Harcourt

Orlando   Boston   Dallas   Chicago   San Diego

Visit *The Learning Site!*

www.harcourtschool.com

Jamie showed his opened journal to his dad. "I did all my homework and my chores," he said. "It's still early."

"Why don't you help me bake a pie?" said his dad. "That will give you something to do."

"What kind of pie, Dad?" Jamie asked.

"How about a cherry pie?" Dad asked.

"I have some ripe cherries from the store."

"Sounds good to me!" said Jamie.

3

"Let's make a list of what we will need to make the pie," said Dad. "You read, and I will write."

Jamie read, "We will need cherries, flour, sugar, and butter."

Jamie and his Dad got out all the things
on their list. They got out bowls, spoons,
and cups, too.

"We need one more tool," said Jamie.
He gave his dad a mixing spoon. "Now
we are ready to bake!"

"You know, it takes a lot of people to make a pie," said Dad.

"What do you mean, Dad?" asked Jamie. "Baking a pie seems like a pretty simple thing to do."

6

Dad held up the bag of flour. He asked Jamie, "Where do you think flour comes from?"

"I think it comes from plants," said Jamie.

"Farmers plant wheat," said Dad. "The seeds sprout and grow into plants like tall grass. The grain from the wheat is sent to mills to be ground into flour. The flour is shipped to stores."

"What about butter, Dad?" asked
Jamie. "Where does butter come from?"
"Butter is made from milk," said Dad.
"You know that milk comes from cows."

"The milk is sent to a dairy and put into large tubs. An engine stirs and stirs the milk until it turns into butter."

"What about sugar, Dad?" asked
Jamie, "Where does sugar come from?"
"Sugar comes from the sugarcane
plant," said Dad.

"Farmers plant sugarcane too," said Dad. "These plants grow tall and strong. Sugarcane farmers cut the stems. The sugar is in the stems of the plants."

"I heard that cherries grow on trees. Is that right?" asked Jamie.

"Cherries do grow on cherry trees," said Dad. "Every spring, flowers grow on the trees. Cherries begin to grow inside the flowers. After the flowers fall off, the cherries grow until they are ripe."

"Many workers earn money by picking the cherries off the trees. The cherries are then shipped to stores."

"I never knew it took so many people to make a pie," said Jaime. "I learned a lot!"

"We couldn't have made this pie without them," said Dad.

"The best thing about baking a pie is working alongside you, Dad," said Jamie.

"Eating the pie alongside you is pretty good, too," said Dad.

Think and Respond

1 Where does this story take place?

2 How does Jamie learn that making a pie is not as simple as it seems?

3 What new things did you learn?

4 How do you know that Jamie and his dad love one another?

5 How are the things they use for the pie alike? How are they different?

6 What kind of pie would you like to make? Why?

Read Measurements Make a pie! List how much of each thing is needed.

School-Home Connection Find some kitchen measuring tools. Which ones measure solids? Which ones measure liquids?

Word Count: 445

ISBN 0-15-323077-0